The Omnibus Publishing
5422 Ebenezer Rd., PO Box 152
Baltimore, MD 21162

www.theomnibuspublishing.com

Publisher's Note: This is a work of fiction. Names, characters, places, and incidents are a product of the author's imagination. Locales and public names are sometimes used for atmospheric purposes. Any resemblance to actual people, living or dead, or to businesses, companies, events, institutions, or locales is completely coincidental.

Book design © 2018, BookDesignTemplates.com

Ordering Information: Special discounts are available on quantity purchases by corporations, associations, and others. For details, contact the publisher at the address above.

Baltimore / Shreya Hessler, Psy.D. — First Edition

ISBN 978-0-9986811-4-6

Printed in the United States of America

For Bianca, Jai, Bella, and Jason for being my world.

And for JW for the inspiration for this journey.

BIANCA FINDS HER BOUNCE

By Shreya Hessler, Psy.D.

Illustrated by Fanny Liem

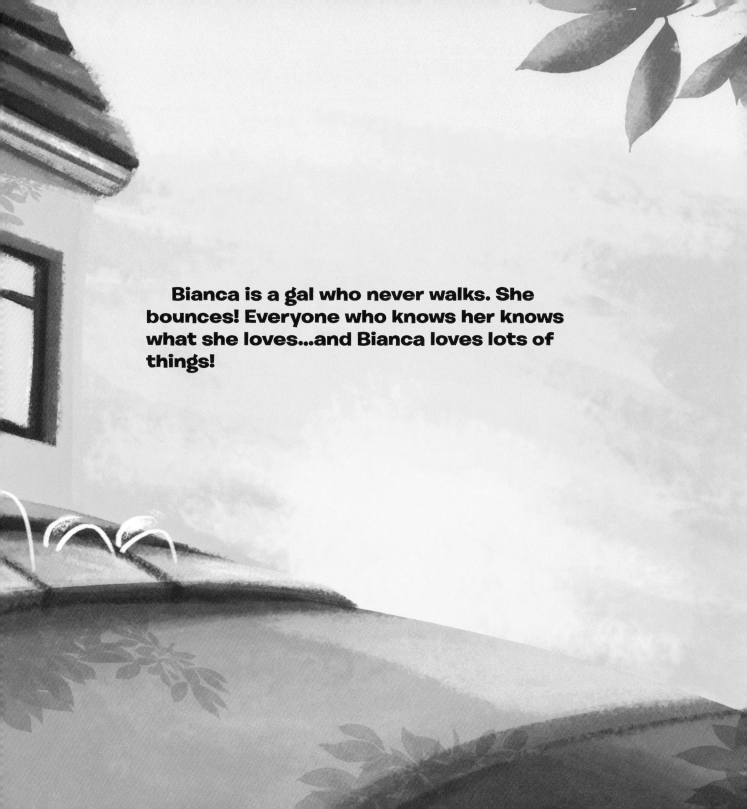

Bianca is a gal who never walks. She bounces! Everyone who knows her knows what she loves...and Bianca loves lots of things!

She loves to blow bubbles with her brother outside.
"Look how big mine is Bianca!" her little brother squeals.

Reading books about faraway places...

...with incredible adventures, makes her happy.

Bianca adores beautiful baskets to keep the flowers that she picks from her momma's garden.

Ballet class brings her joy because it is where

she can twirl,

and twirl,

and twirl!

While her loves are many, there is one thing that Bianca does *NOT* love, and that is BACON. Her mother makes sure bacon is never on her plate at breakfast in the morning.

There came a day when Momma began to notice a change in her daughter.
Bianca was not loving things as much as she usually does.

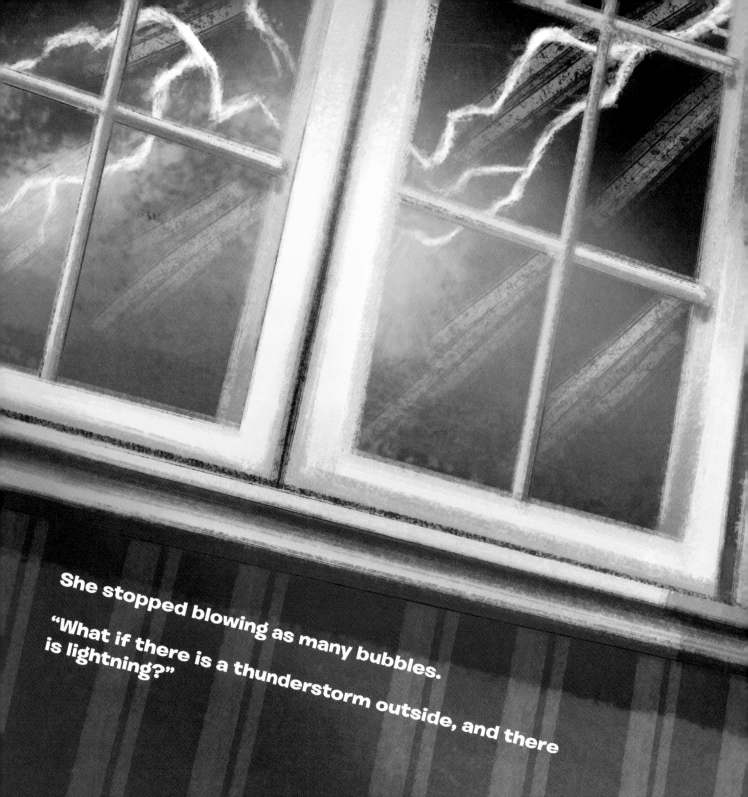

She stopped blowing as many bubbles. "What if there is a thunderstorm outside, and there is lightning?"

She put away her books.

"What if there is a scary part in the story and I have a bad dream?"

Bianca even quit twirling in ballet class.

"What if I fall and get hurt and can't dance?"

Bianca lost her bounce!

One night at bedtime, the not so bouncy Bianca and her momma have a long talk.

"What's been going on Bianca? You've lost your bounce."

Sighing, Bianca replies, "Momma, I have been thinking about a lot of bad stuff and I can't stop thinking about it. I have a lot of worries."

Her momma gave her a big hug. "Bianca, it sounds like you're frying bacon."

Bianca didn't understand, "What do my worries have to do with bacon?"

"Well, do you like bacon?"

"No, I don't like it," Bianca replies, making a yucky face. "It makes me feel funny."

"Now tell me, do you like the worries you have been feeling?" says momma.

Bianca grimaces, "No, I don't like them either. They make me feel funny too."

"Every time you dwell on these worries, it's like you are sizzling bacon in a pan. Maybe when the worries come, we can imagine you are taking the frying pan off the stove and the sizzle will stop."

Looking thoughtfully at her mom, Bianca asks, "How do I do that?"

Momma replies, "How about when you feel your worries creeping into your thoughts, you can tell me that you are frying bacon? We can write down your worries, talk it out, and discover a solution. This way, the worry is out of your head so you don't get stuck, or sizzle, on it long. That's just like taking the frying pan off the stove."

"Will that make my worries go away forever?" hopes Bianca.

"If we can get the thoughts out of your head, it will be like the bacon won't sizzle as much. The worries are thoughts. It doesn't mean they will come true.

Always remember, if something you worry about does happen, we can deal with it together."

The next morning, Bianca sits down for breakfast and Momma hands her some pink and red paper. They look like bacon strips.

Bianca asks, "What's this?"

Mamma smiles and says, "When you have a worry, write it down on one of these strips of papers. Then we can talk out a solution or simply place it in recycling."

Bianca places the strips in her pocket. That afternoon, her brother asks her to blow bubbles in the backyard. Clouds are gathering, and Bianca begins to worry about thunderstorms.

She remembers the bacon strips in her pocket, reaches inside and pulls one out. She writes her worry on a strip.

Bianca wonders, *What if it storms and there is lightning?*

She thinks a moment about a solution and realizes, *If it does, I'll go inside!*

Excited, she runs to her mom. "Momma! I was just frying some bacon and I took it off the stove!"

Her mom grinned, "Do you think you can go outside and play with your brother?"

Bianca replied, "Yes! I'll take my bacon strips with me!"

"That's my girl!"

And that's how Bianca found her bounce!

Bianca still loves to blow bubbles, read books,

collect flowers in her basket,

...and twirl in ballet.

Occasionally Bianca still fries bacon. When that happens, she will write down the worry onto a bacon strip and place it in a box. Sometimes she shares them with her mom and sometimes she does not. But she never keeps the bacon on the stove.

THE END

ABOUT THE AUTHOR

Shreya Hessler, Psy.D.

Dr. Hessler is the founder and director of The MINDset Center. She has been in private practice for over a decade. She specializes in the identification and treatment of anxiety disorders, attention deficit-hyperactivity disorder, depression, and behavioral disorders. Dr. Hessler is trained in cognitive-behavioral and applied behavioral therapy for the treatment of children, adolescents, and adults. She uses a comprehensive approach in working with clients. After a thorough diagnostic interview, clients collaborate with Dr. Hessler to create a treatment plan that target specific symptoms.

http://www.mindsetcenter.com

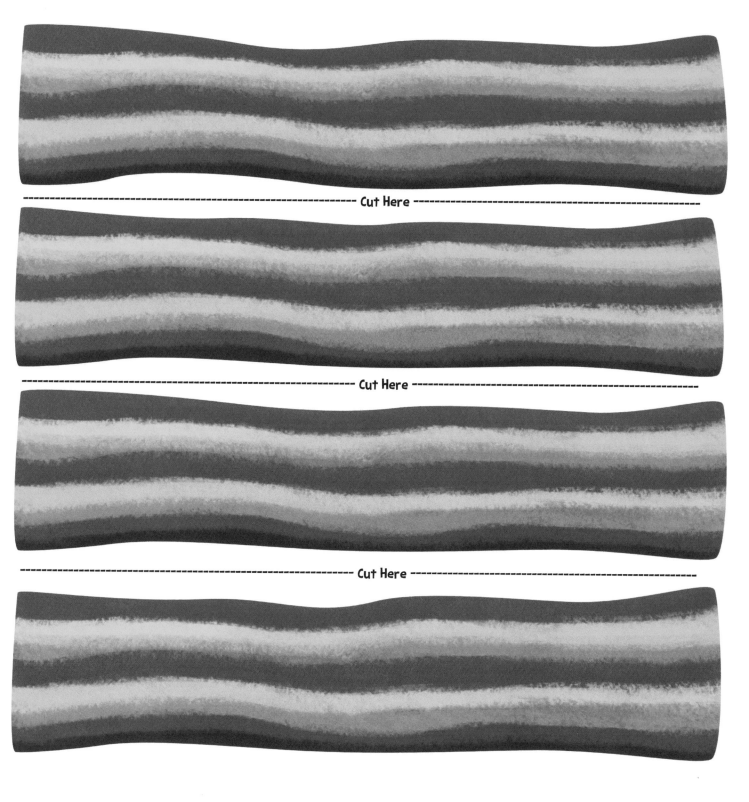

----------------------------------- Cut Here -----------------------------------

----------------------------------- Cut Here -----------------------------------

----------------------------------- Cut Here -----------------------------------

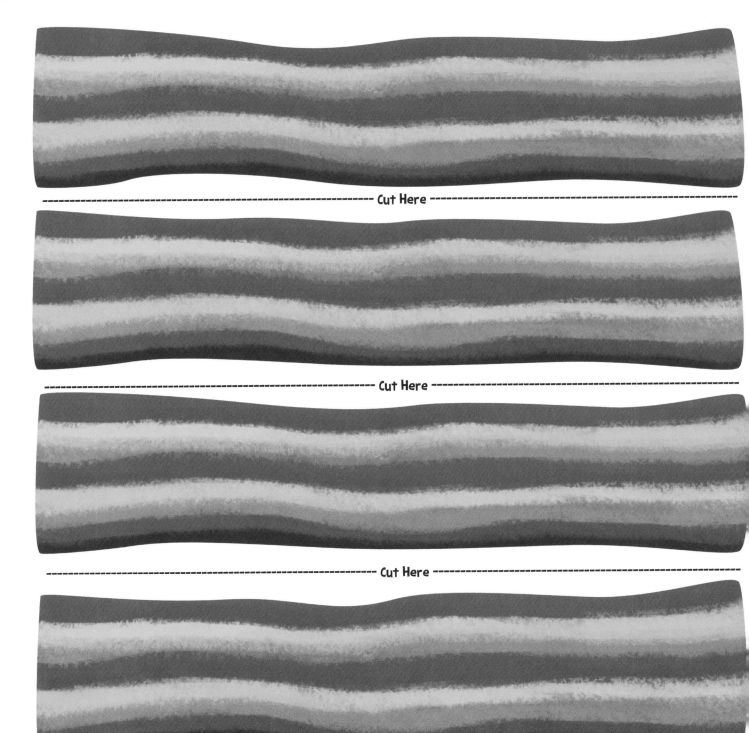

------------------------------ Cut Here ------------------------------

------------------------------ Cut Here ------------------------------

------------------------------ Cut Here ------------------------------

CPSIA information can be obtained at www.ICGtesting.com
Printed in the USA
BVIW12n0244250118
505534BV00007B/18